Translation copyright © 2020 by Dupuis
Cover art and interior illustrations copyright © 2018, 2020 by Dupuis

Published in the United States by RH Graphic, an imprint of Random House Children's Books, a division of Penguin Random House LLC, New York. The titles in this work were originally published in two separate volumes in the French language in Belgium as *Aubépine 1: Le génie saligaud*, copyright © 2018 Dupuis by Thom Pico & Karensac, and *Aubépine 2: Le renard furax*, copyright © 2018 Dupuis by Thom Pico & Karensac, by Éditions Dupuis S.A., Marcinelle, in 2018. All rights reserved.

RH Graphic with the book design is a trademark of Penguin Random House LLC.

Visit us on the Web! RHKidsGraphic.com • @RHKidsGraphic

Educators and librarians, for a variety of teaching tools, visit us at RHTeachersLibrarians.com

Library of Congress Cataloging-in-Publication Data
Names: Pico, Thom, author. | Karensac, illustrator. | Smith, Owen (Owen M.), translator. | Smith, Anne Collins, translator. | Pico, Thom. Génie saligaud. English. | Pico, Thom. Renard furax. English.
Title: Aster and the accidental magic / Thom Pico and Karensac ; translated by Anne and Owen Smith.
Description: First Random House Graphic edition. | New York : Random House Graphic, an imprint of Random House Children's Books, a division of Penguin Random House LLC, 2020. | "Originally published in two volumes, Aubépine 1: Le génie saligaud, and Aubépine 2: Le renard furax, in France by Dupuis in 2018." | Summary: Aster is bored at her new home in the mountains in the middle of nowhere—until she meets an odd old shepherdess and her woolly dogs, a sneaky trickster, and an angry fox.
Identifiers: LCCN 2019014042 (print) | LCCN 2019017516 (ebook) | ISBN 978-0-593-11886-3 (ebook) | ISBN 978-0-593-12417-8 (hardcover) ISBN 978-0-593-11884-9 (trade) | ISBN 978-0-593-11885-6 (lib. bdg.)
Subjects: LCSH: Graphic novels. | CYAC: Graphic novels. | Country life—Fiction. | Dogs—Fiction. | Foxes—Fiction. | Genies—Fiction. | Magic—Fiction.
Classification: LCC PZ7.7.P523 (ebook) | LCC PZ7.7.P523 As 2020 (print) | DDC 741.5/944—dc23

Designed by Patrick Crotty
Translated by Anne and Owen Smith
Thanks to Gina and Anton

MANUFACTURED IN CHINA
10 9 8 7 6 5 4 3 2 1
First American Edition

A comic on every bookshelf.

Aster
AND THE
ACCIDENTAL MAGIC

Story and Script
THOM PICO

Story and Art
KARENSAC

To Julien, Guillaume, Bola, Élisa,
Laurence, Stéphane, and Jonathan

Aster

MAKES SOME
POORLY THOUGHT-THROUGH WISHES

CLAK

Stupid Reed... him and his stories about monsters...I bet he just didn't want to get stuck here with me.

PLOP

CLICK

And don't forget, the great migration will occur next Saturday evening.

During this emergency, we advise all affected residents to evacuate to designated shelters or barricade yourselves indoors.

Fear is gripping the region, and even though the revolutionary Robo-Bird project is advancing quickly, the big question is—will it be ready in time?

We posed the question to the project director, Professor Rose...

Same old story! Migration here, migration there! It's getting ridiculous!

I can't believe people are getting so freaked out over a few birds.

ZAP

MOM?

Yes, sweetie?

The TV keeps talking about how the crows are gonna come and destroy everything...

Yes, I know, sweetie.

Did we really come here just because of this cruddy migration?

It's my job.

So, how are you going to stop them? Are you making a killer robot or what?

It's more complicated than that, sweetie.

Why not kill them? Aren't they mean?

Listen to me carefully, dear. It's not the birds' fault.

Later that day...

When are we going back to the city?

I'm not quite done yet, sweetie.

I miss my friends.

You'll make new friends at school.

School?! What do you mean? I thought we were only staying for a few weeks!

Um... that's what I meant!

Besides, who can I make friends with? Nobody lives here but old fossils...

You shouldn't talk that way...they're not so old.

· · · ·

Okay, it's true that the village is deserted, but if all goes well, everyone will return in a few days!

Besides, there are some really interesting people around here. The shepherds, for example. When I was little, everyone kept praising them for protecting the mountain during the migrations.

And how will they defend themselves against giant angry birds? That's stupid.

Don't ask me—it's some sort of tradition.

Actually, it's a form of cultural atavism arising from the region's isolation. You know, like insular conduct.

What did she say?

Just smile and nod.

I will admit, it feels weird to be here. I haven't been back since our house was destroyed in the last migration. I wonder if the granny with the woolly dogs is still here.

Well, I doubt she's still alive. She was already as old as dirt when I was a kid!

It's not cool to make fun of fossils, Dad.

YIP!!!

Heyyy!

29

Hello?

Ma'am... are you dead?

Not a chance!

Um... congrats?

Sorry, I didn't mean to bother you. See you later—maybe.

Wait a moment, child.

Do you like the mountain?

Um...it's really pretty.

I think the mountain likes you too.

Really? Um... that's nice.

The mountain doesn't like just anybody. It won't even recognize some people whose families have lived here for generations. They'd never be able to find their way here—but you did.

But I got here by accident...

Hmm...by accident, you say? There are hidden corners on this mountain that few people can find—certainly not those who run away every time the birds migrate. Only those who are guided by the mountain.

I can tell you're not from around here, but you're no ordinary girl—you have the mountain inside you.

Uh, okaaay. Would you happen to be one of the old shepherds that my dad told me about? The ones who protect the valley, I mean?

By the wind's twelve quarters! No one's ever called me old before. Nowadays, there's no one left to protect the mountain but me.

Well, you don't have to worry—my mother is going to fix everything! She's an ornithologist, and she is too smart to foul up.

I see...you won't hold it against me if I stay on guard, will you?

Tell me, do you like my dogs? They're woolly!

Well...they are pretty cute.

I always say, there's nothing better for guarding a mountain than a woolly dog. I tell you what...take that little one there.

YIP!

He's very nice, but his coat won't grow. He'll never be any good for wool. But he'll make you a good companion.

YIP!

I'd love to, but I can't! My parents would never agree.

Parents only see what they want to see and only know what they want to know. You're lonely—I can tell. He'll be a good friend, and with him at your side, the mountain will always look after you.

Now take him and be on your way. You have far to travel if you wish to return home before nightfall.

But...

Er, well...thank you! See you later...

I hope so.

So, we're going to spend a lot of time together!

YIP!

The next day...

YIP!

37

Doesn't exactly inspire confidence, does it?

Right?

OKAY, LISTEN. I'VE BEEN THE TRICKSTER SPIRIT OF THIS CLEARING FOR QUITE SOME TIME NOW, AND WHEN YOU SPEND SEVERAL CENTURIES GRANTING THE WISHES OF PASSERSBY, SOONER OR LATER YOU RUN INTO A MALCONTENT WHO'S NEVER SATISFIED AND VENTS HIS FRUSTRATION BY GIVING YOU A ROTTEN NAME!

So why don't you change it?

Okay.

What? Don't you think I'd change it if I could? Once a spirit's been given a name, it's over and done. The name sticks forever. So if you don't mind, let's just drop the subject.

Thanks.

If you don't mind...

RAA AAH

Fine! What's your first wish?

I get wishes?

Of course! All trickster spirits are contractually obligated to grant wishes.

THREE WISHES*

*Standard rules and restrictions apply!

FIRST: No do-overs! You can't use one wish to cancel another wish.

SECOND: keep your wishes out of my backyard!

No wishes can affect my clearing.

THIRD: Wait your turn! I serve only one client at a time.

Although nobody ever comes out here, so it's not usually a problem.

Wow! You have an awful lot of rules.

Well, I give awful service! Or is it awesome service? I forget. First wish, please! The end-user agreement requires immediate activation.

This is all a bit sudden...I'm just not sure...

It's not hard! What do you need right now?

Well...a friend to talk to.

How sad!

It'll be okay. I'm sure I'll learn a lot from you, Rapscallion!

YIP!

I want to be able to speak with Buzz!

Are you quite sure?

Yes!

I have no idea what just happened.

Well, it didn't meet the criteria for a hallucination.

Are you sure? It was too bizarre to be real.

Trust me, dreams about pit-dwelling magic tricksters who grant wishes are well beyond the capacity of most dogs. As a rule, we dream about dead squirrels.

I imagine so.

Wait...

YOU CAN TALK?!

Of course.

HOW BRILLIANT!

Really?

We'll be best friends and talk about all sorts of things—we'll have a great time together!

I thought we were best friends already.

You know, we can have good times together without talking.

True...but it's just not the same.

It's rather unusual for dogs to spend much time discussing matters. We prefer showing our feelings rather than talking about them. That's why dogs get along so much better than people.

Oh man! I can't believe it—a talking dog who's smart! Imagine the possibilities!

Reed is gonna be so jealous!

It's getting late...shouldn't we be heading home?

Holy cow! I can't believe it's night already! We'll have to hurry!

Ssshhh...

ASTER!

Aster! Where have you been? We've been worried sick about you!

You need to spend less time outdoors...

BARK! YIP YIP ARF WOOF!

(Sorry! I'll go straight to bed. Love you!)

What just happened?

It appears she's expressing her contrariety with regard to the upheavals of the recent past by means of zoomorphism. It's not uncommon in kids her age.

Ask a silly question... We'll have to have a serious talk with her tomorrow...

Indubitably.

Am I mistaken, or did she have a little dog?

I didn't notice.

Greetings, mortal!
What would you like
for your second wish?

I wish my parents had
never moved here!

Is that exactly how
you want to phrase
your wish?

What, that's it?

Look, I've been trying to tell you—you can never trust trickster spirits! They'll grant your wishes, all right, but they'll take your words literally so you don't get what you want...

Basically, they're just mean!

Oh no! I'm sorry, Buzz...

I'm an idiot... why do I do such stupid things?

Don't feel so bad...you're only human.

Well, hello, my dear! What are you doing here?

...

Are you mute? Oh, I'm sorry.

Yip?

I see! You don't speak our language! Don't worry. It doesn't matter. If you're hungry, you can join us for dinner.

Francis, my love! Dinnertime!

But they're monsters!

Well, monsters are people too. If there are any sausages in that soup, I'd love to have one.

This can't be happening! I want my parents back! What if these monsters have eaten them?

HAHAHA HA

Such a nice couple? I highly doubt it.

Well, suppose my parents never left the city, and these monsters still live here. Why am I here?

YAAAAH

KRIAA

ROAR

POW

ROAR

Oh my stars! What are you two doing here?!

Yap! Grrr yap yap woof yip!

(Help us! We're trying to get everything back to normal!)

Yip!

By the wind's twelve quarters, child, I can't understand a word you're saying! Stand back—I have a mountain to protect.

Is she...?

Yes! I think so!

I'm the reason she's dead. If only I hadn't made those silly wishes...

If Mom had been here with her robot, none of this would have happened.

It's not Granny's fault. It's not even the birds' fault. I'm the one who's responsible...

I'm afraid we have no choice but to seek Rapscallion's help. If you phrase your last wish properly, perhaps he can set everything straight.

Sniffle

Let's go.

Well, well, well. Once again, the chosen one graces me with her presence. Has everything gone as you wished?

Stop making fun of me!

Me? Make fun of you? Never! All I did was give you exactly what you wished for.

You must have read stories about tricksters—we all behave the same way. It's not our fault humans never remember what they read.

Nothing turned out the way I wanted!

How was I supposed to guess what you wanted? I'm just a trickster—not Google.

But a person is dead!

So what? Fate is not a toy for you to play with. Choices have consequences. You should know that by now.

It's not my responsibility that your wishes ended up killing somebody!

I know...

So...do you want your third wish, or have you just come to vent about your poor choices?

Hold on— I'm thinking.

Choose your words carefully— you won't have another chance!

Buzz, I have a plan. Do you trust me?

Well... I suppose so. What's the plan?

A magician never reveals her secrets. Hang on, things might get a bit rough.

Aster

GETS A MAGICAL FOX
EXCEEDINGLY UPSET

Hmm...trouble's coming. I can sense it...

Hey, new kid! Wanna come play by the river with me and my buddies?

Thanks for asking, but I already have plans.

Suit yourself! Say, will your dog be waiting for you again today?

Of course—he can tell time.

Hey, don't try to con me...

Welcome home!

Is school over already? How about a video game?

Thanks, Dad, but I'd rather take a walk.

Again?! You're never home anymore—you're always outside!

You can't spare even a little time for your old dad?

ONE PLAYER

YIIIIIP

Yoo-hoo! Granny! Where are you?

Handling this summer's bird migration doesn't give you the right to call me Granny, child.

Yikes! Where did you come from?

Never you mind. What brings you out this way?

Nothing in particular... I just haven't seen you for a while.

It's not a good day for a visit.

Gently, dogs, gently!

Something's not quite right, and I don't want you underfoot if there's a problem.

Oh! Is there anything I can do? I'd like to help if I can.

It's kind of you to offer, but my troubles are my own. Even if, as you say, You managed to trick Rapscallion into bringing me back to life.

Why are you so worried?

It's autumn. Any moment now, autumn will arrive.

You know I'm very fond of her, Buzz, but she loves to make mountains out of molehills.

YIP!

Buzz, although I can't speak Dog anymore, you still seem to understand everything I say.

I sure could use your advice now, but there's no way I'm ever going back to that Rapscallion of a trickster spirit again!

We shall see...

Well, Dad, what have we here?

Whole pan-seared trout with broccoli and stewed squid!

Um...okay. But why?

Well, since you're at school all day, your mother's off in the wilderness somewhere studying birds, and your brother's away at college, I thought I might finally learn how to cook...

It's a great idea, Dad. But how about starting with something less, well, exotic?

You needn't be so quarrelsome. The Queen of Spring, after all, is always courteous.

If she wants to be all sweetness and light when you meet, that's her affair. I'm not interested in any small talk—just give me the crown!

Your feeble attempts to delay the inevitable infuriate me!

You become more ill-mannered every year... My time is over. The crown is yours!

Heh, heh. Silent but deadly...

AAAOOOOOUUUHHHH

ASTER!

For heaven's sake, Aster, wake up!

Just five more minutes, Buzz...

BUZZ?!

Did you just talk?

I'll explain later! Come on! It's an emergency!

Buzz?

Wait!

SCRRR

BAM

What's going on, Buzz? You have to tell me!

It's Granny! She must be in mortal peril! The big dogs have been howling continuously for an hour!

Oh no! She's not dead again, is she?

I don't know, but I hope she's not going to make it a habit!

AAAAOOOOUUUUUUHHHHHHHHH

GRANNY!

She's still breathing! But she needs medical care—I'll call an ambulance right away!

BONK

Let's not get carried away. Help me get to my cabin. I have everything I need there.

B-b-but...

And stop stammering! You sound like a sheep—and I loathe those filthy beasts!

Click

136

Aster, let's head home. We're in the way here.

If the dogs don't need my help caring for her, why did they summon me?

Um...Does it matter? We prefer not to speak of it...even among ourselves.

I'm not in the mood for riddles.

Well, it's just...

While we dogs are very intelligent, we are occasionally vexed by...doors...

Doors?

Yes, doors. The concept is simple, and we understand them in theory, but we lack certain...appendages, you see.

Oh.

Well, when you put it that way, it makes perfect sense.

Really? You don't find it ridiculous?

Nah.

By the way, when were you going to tell me that you can speak Human?

I had acquired a taste for talking with you, and I missed our chats. So I devised a way to remedy the situation.

Don't tell me you did something stupid, like going to see the trickster Rapscallion!

Don't disparage my plan! I formulated my second wish precisely, and voilà! We can talk.

So why didn't you tell me sooner?

I was waiting for just the right moment. I know how sensitive you get whenever trickster spirits are mentioned.

You're not angry with me, are you? We're still friends?

.TWIP.

Silly.

TING

TING

ZAP

FLIP

The Chestnut Knights

HULL

LEAF

BURR

Uh... yeah...

I couldn't sleep, so I went out for a little walk.

Oh?

You need to be careful, Aster—it can be dangerous outside.

Chill out, Dad! Giant bird season is over!

Hmm...

SLURP

SLURP

AH!

Okay, time for another walk.

Think again, young lady!

Wait, what?

It's a school day, isn't it?

Wait— isn't it Saturday?

"Nice try, Aster! I may not have a job, but I still know what day it is! And if I'm not mistaken, Friday is a school day!" Blah blah blah.

Argh! I was so sure it was the weekend!

Weird...

Where is everyone?

Wait—it really is Saturday! ARGH! Bravo, Dad!

Way to go, Mr. "I Still Know What Day It Is!"

TAP TAP

SCREECH

So, whatcha doin' here, new kid?

It's silly, but I thought we had school today...

Of course there's no school today—we're on break, duh!

I guess when you skip school for weeks at a time, it's easy to lose track of the schedule!

HUH?

HA HA HA HA

?

149

First of all, let me make one thing clear: this valley is unlike any other place in the world!

For ages untold, a being of immense power has been imprisoned here. And yet, although he remains bound, his magic seeps out!

Whoa... who is this superpowered being?

That is a story for another time. As I was saying, a great enchantment was forged to confine this being's power, and four guardians were appointed— the sovereigns of the four seasons!

Since then, to fulfill their duty and protect the valley, the kings and queens of spring, summer, autumn, and winter wield in turn the Crown of Seasons!

The what?

153

The Crown of Seasons!

The Crown of Seasons isolates this being and controls his magic. The valley and its inhabitants remain safe only because we wield this power!

What do you mean by "we"? Are you...?

HEE HEE

Yes! I am the Queen of Summer!

But...how is that possible?

Long ago, the Queen of Summer was no different from the other sovereigns. She was wise, however, and when the first human settlers began establishing their homesteads here...

...she alone recognized the necessity of integrating humans into their great enterprise.

The only way to accomplish this goal, she knew, was to abdicate and pass on her powers to a human. She chose an enthusiastic young shepherd girl...me.

And so, for eight hundred years, I have reigned as Queen of Summer.

Yes, you. I suspect that one of the wishes you made to the trickster Rapscallion has upset the apple cart, as it were.

When I died in the other reality, you must have become the new Queen of Summer!

OH!

It wouldn't be such a bother— only you brought my staff back into the new reality.

Now the power of the crown has become fragmented, divided among you, me, and our staffs. The strain is too great, and the valley is being overwhelmed by raw magic.

The first sign of trouble is the appearance of time bubbles—fractures in time itself. Unless we act quickly, even more dire consequences will follow.

Okay...so what's the plan?

The first step is to reunify the power of the crown. I need you to scurry back to your house as quickly as possible and retrieve your staff.

We have uncovered vital information! If the staff thingy has magic power, the boss will want it right away! It's our job to get it before the snot-nosed kid does!

...

YES, CHIEF!

CLAK

What's the next step?

Once we have both staffs, you abdicate in my favor, I pass the crown to the king of Autumn, and this whole unfortunate incident will be over.

Just like that?

Just like that.

Great, let's go! There's not a moment to lose!

Is it me, or did that puppy just speak Human?

Human, tell us what we want to know! We are the Chest—

The Chestnut knights! I don't believe it!

Huh?

OMG! OMG! You're real! I heard tons of stories about you when I was growing up! You were my heroes! I'm your number-one fan! You are so cool!

Really? I had no idea we were famous...

Are you kidding?

Burr, the warrior who dreams of becoming a tree!

...

The mysterious Hull, whose every word is a gift!

And Leaf, their honorable and intrepid chief! You're real! It's all true!

Um...thanks. That's nice. Do you know where your daughter's staff is?

No idea. I can never keep track of where she keeps her stuff. Why?

SILENCE! WE'RE ASKING THE QUESTIONS!

SO WHAT NOW, CHIEF?

We take him to the boss.

After the fox gets done with him, he won't have any secrets left. Besides, we can use him as a hostage. Chestnut knights—forward!

The Chestnut knights have taken me hostage! So cool!

Am I seeing what I think I see—a bird frozen in flight?

We'd better hurry—matters are getting worse.

Terrible...

...isn't it?

Whoa!

You're the Queen of Summer's friend, aren't you? I've been keeping an eye on you.

Let there be no mistake. If I don't get the crown soon, everything will be reduced to dust.

I hope she's told you—this is only the beginning!

I...

Silence, human!

Go immediately to the old hag.

Tell her that I won't let her destroy the valley! I will get my crown—one way or another!

Autumn will have his due!

Yes, in fact...

PooF

ARGH! People who won't listen really tick me off!

Come on, Buzz, we're almost home!

All set— let's go!

WHAT???

The other part of the crown is in the possession of that snot-nosed kid?!

Fools! If you hadn't dawdled, I'd have the crown already!

Well, boss, we did take her father hostage. That's something, isn't it?

We can't waste time on negotiation. Raw magic is about to tear the valley apart. Kill him! And then let's go get that staff.

Um...excuse me?

HEY, BOSS, THIS GUY AIN'T SO BAD! THERE'S NO NEED TO OFF HIM!

How dare you?

My brother is right—he's harmless. We should let him go.

Listen up, pip-squeaks! The humans have violated the agreement! They deserve no mercy!

He's a human! So cut his throat!

But, boss...

But nothing!

Snick

I'm rather fond of this human.

All right—bring him along. He can be your servant!

The Chestnut knights saved my life... Too cool!

Oh no! Granny! The dogs!

I can't believe it! What do we do now?

SNIFF

Aster, I've found something. This way!

What on earth is he?

I have no idea, but he carries your father's scent!

POKE

Hey, you! On your feet!

What exactly are you doing here?

I am Leaf, Captain of the Chestnut knights, in the service of the fox, king of Autumn.

Well, I'm Aster, Interim Co-Sovereign of Summer, and you're going to tell me what I want to know!

Where's my father? And Granny?

Lady Aster, we had planned to exchange your father for your staff and thus force the other Queen of Summer to give us her power.

But nothing went according to plan.

CLING

By the time we arrived, a time bubble had engulfed her cabin, greatly accelerating the passage of time.

Everything was in ruins; the only thing left was her staff, the twin of the one you now carry. I'm sorry—I fear your friend is dead.

Our boss was exceedingly upset, because without the crown, he thought it would be impossible for him to begin his reign.

Okay—I see. Makes sense.

Really?

Of course not! Nothing makes sense! Why does he want to involve the Queen of Spring? Weren't things complicated enough already?!

I think he hopes to save us by wielding the power of another Sovereign of the Seasons! But all he'll do is destroy the balance of nature!

By killing spring, the fox can stop the time bubbles, but only by destroying the valley!

Okay, then we need to stop him. That much is clear. But why is he taking my father along?

If he fails, the fox will need your father to serve as a receptacle to recover the power of the Queen of Spring.

That's not so bad...

Of course, your father will die, but the fox is risking his own life in this process.

Holy cow! Well, don't just stand there! Where do we find the Queen of Spring?

Allow me to be your guide! Henceforth, I place myself at your service, my lady!

Well...okay. Sounds good!

This way!

Wow!

187

It seems I arrived not a moment too soon!

The old woman! But how?!

You are too predictable to outfox me. My brave doggies sensed the danger and led me to safety before my cabin collapsed.

If you cease your foolishness, king of Autumn, there's a way we can save everyone.

Rats.

TAP

Okay, if I'm not mistaken, I'm now the Queen of Summer.

Would you like to declare a truce? There's no need for war when we can negotiate...

NO! The only thing you humans want is power—I will never trust you! I SHALL TAKE THE CROWN FROM YOUR DEAD BODY!

What do we do now, Aster?

Well...I've won, haven't I? I'm the Queen of Summer.

Alas, my lady, you are too inexperienced to wield such power. And the fox is in no condition...

Hey! Mr. King of Winter!

Yes?

How would you like to receive the Crown of Seasons a little ahead of schedule?

Well, I'm surprised! Still, perhaps it's for the best!

The king of Autumn was mistaken about you humans.

PooF

Tell me, honey, do you have adventures like this every time you take a walk?

Not exactly, Dad. Some days are better than others. Today was... not bad.

Really? Uh...you still need to be careful!

Hello, Granny! How are you?

Well enough. Come over here, child. The king of Winter certainly hasn't wasted any time.

Oh, it's not so bad! At least we can have a calm discussion with him.

By the way, my father has finally found a job!

Really? What?

He is writing the chronicles of the Chestnut knights!

Good for him. Now hold out your hands—I have a gift for you.

Oh!

Do you want me to take care of him?

I'm too old for such nonsense. He has to regain his full strength before next autumn.

He must also learn to appreciate humans.

~Yawn

It's a big responsibility, but I have faith in you.

208

Now that I think about it, Granny, why are there no sheep here in the valley? Everywhere else, wool comes from sheep, not dogs.

My child, that is a long story, a long story indeed...

Aster and the Accidental Magic was thumbnailed with pen on paper, then inked and colored in Photoshop. The book is lettered in Hawthorn.

THE CHARACTERS OF ASTER

ASTER

BUZZ

Aster has a strong personality for a ten-year-old. As a city dweller, she is NOT enthusiastic about the idea of moving to the mountains. But she can't resist the call of adventure, and it looks like this nowhere town might have more than enough excitement for Aster and her new friends.

Buzz is a small woolly dog who doesn't have wool. He's Aster's closest and most loyal friend, and was given to her by Granny. It turns out that he's really chatty, as Aster quickly finds out once he gains the ability to talk.

MOM

DAD

Aster's mother is a well-known ornithologist (person who knows a lot about birds) who moved her family to the mountains so she could continue her studies and stop the invasion of giant destructive crows. She tends to analyze every situation with a scientific approach.

Aster's father has quit his job to follow his family to the middle of nowhere. Since he grew up in the mountains, he knows a little about the environment...and some of the characters Aster might come across. Too bad he can't help being bored to death anyway.

GRANNY

THE TRICKSTER RAPSCALLION

Who is that mysterious old shepherdess who keeps giving Aster weird advice? And why does she have woolly dogs instead of sheep?

One of the oldest and most powerful spirits of the universe...beware of the wishes he grants! He is good at twisting other people's words for his own amusement.

THE KING
OF AUTUMN

THE KING
OF WINTER

The king of Autumn is a fox who means business. Despite his good intentions for the countryside, his hatred of humans stops him from finding a peaceful solution.

The king of Winter is a mountain. He takes up a lot of space, but he is good-natured and has a great sense of humor. Nobody knows where he comes from, but it's clear that he's been around for a very long time.

THE CHESTNUT KNIGHTS

HULL   **LEAF**   **BURR**

The Chestnut knights are legendary mountain warriors who follow their hearts. They might be in service to the king of Autumn, but that doesn't mean they can't make up their own minds about the situations they find themselves in.

Aster

BUZZ AND The CHESTNUT KNIGHTS

will return in...

RH
GRAPHIC

RH GRAPHIC
THE DEBUT LIST

BUG BOYS
By Laura Knetzger

Bugs, friends, the world around us—this book has everything!
Come explore *Bug Boys* for the fun, thoughtful adventure of growing up and being yourself.

Chapter Book

THE RUNAWAY PRINCESS
By Johan Troïanowski

The castle is quiet.
And dull.
And boring.
Escape on a quest for excitement with our runaway princess, Robin!

Middle-Grade

ASTER AND THE ACCIDENTAL MAGIC
By Thom Pico & Karensac

Nothing fun ever happens in the middle of the country . . . except maybe . . . magic?
That's just the beginning of absolutely everything going wrong for Aster.

Middle-Grade

WITCHLIGHT
By Jessi Zabarsky

Lelek doesn't have any friends or family in the world. And then she meets Sanja. Swords, magic, falling in love . . . these characters come together in a journey to heal the wounds of the past.

Young Adult

FIND US ONLINE AT @RHKIDSGRAPHIC AND RHKIDSGRAPHIC.COM